SINBAD
The Runaway

Home Farm Twins

Sinbad

The Runaway

Jenny Oldfield

Illustrated by Kate Aldous

Hodder
Children's
Books

a division of Hodder Headline plc

A Catalogue record for this book is available from the British Library

ISBN 0 340 66128 3

Typeset by Avon Dataset Ltd, Bidford-on-Avon, Warks

Printed and bound in Great Britain by
Cox & Wyman Ltd, Reading, Berks

Hodder Children's Books
a division of Hodder Headline plc
338 Euston Road
London NW1 3BH

One

'Here, Helen, hold this for me!' David Moore passed a hammer to his daughter. 'And Hannah, just put your hand on this piece of wood while I grab some extra nails.'

The twins were in the farmyard, helping their dad make a rabbit hutch. They worked happily, knowing that Home Farm, their new house in the Lake District, was growing more like a proper farm each day. For a start, they had Speckle the sheepdog. Lucy and Dandy, a pair of geese now poked at the short, dry grass in the field behind the house, and half a dozen shiny brown hens pecked in the yard. Their mum,

1

Mary, took the eggs to the Curlew Cafe in Nesfield where she worked. 'Waste not, want not,' she said.

Mary had rescued the wood for the rabbit hutch from a builders' skip in town. 'If we must have rabbits,' she'd said, 'there's no point spending good money on brand new wood for a hutch.'

'Dad, be quick. My hand's starting to hurt!' Hannah warned. He rummaged in a tin box for some long nails. She tried to hold the two pieces of wood firmly in place.

Helen stood back and stared at the wobbly frame. Would this ever turn into a proper rabbit hutch, she wondered? She grinned at Hannah. Their dad was still learning do-it-yourself the hard way.

'Where are they?' he muttered. He wiped his hands on his crumpled checked shirt, tipped the box upsidedown and rummaged again. 'Just don't let go!'

Hannah did her best. But when Speckle came snuffling with his wet black nose to see what she was up to, she lost her balance and let the wood drop. The frame collapsed in a heap. Speckle jumped back, ears flat, tail drooping.

Helen laughed. 'Speckle thinks he did that, poor thing!'

Hannah turned to her dad. 'Sorry!' She ran one hand through her straight, dark hair.

David Moore stared at the heap of wood. 'Ah well,' he sighed, 'back to the drawing-board!'

They began again with hammer and nails.

'Don't worry, these two rabbits will have the best hutch in Doveton,' he promised. He sawed bits of the wood. The hutch began to take shape.

Helen went to check that the baby rabbits, Sugar and Spice, were safe inside their box in the barn. Luke Martin from the village shop had brought them up to Home Farm. 'Do the twins want a couple of young rabbits to look after?' he'd asked their mum.

Mary Moore had ummed and ahhed, but the twins had taken a peek inside Luke's van and fallen for the rabbits. They turned their big brown eyes on their mum and waited for her reply.

'Oh, OK!' she softened.

'You like animals really!' Helen cried.

'Only you're always saying we don't have time to look after them!' Hannah added.

'I don't,' she insisted.

'But we do!' the twins grinned.

Their dad had agreed to make a home for the

rabbits. Helen and Hannah chalked up another victory. Home Farm was filling up nicely.

'Now all we need is a hutch that doesn't fall apart,' Hannah whispered to Helen when she came back from the barn. 'Dad, shouldn't that piece of wood go across here?' She studied the plan in the DIY book. Then she pointed to a spare plank lying on the flagstones.

He scratched his head. 'Perhaps you're right,' he agreed.

'And shouldn't this one go here?'

He frowned. 'Hmm, maybe.' He put it in place.

She took the book and turned the drawing around. 'And shouldn't it all be this way round?'

'Oh all right, clever clogs!' He hammered away. Soon the hutch began to look like a hutch.

The sun came out from behind white clouds as a fresh wind blew from Doveton Fell. The wind brought down a shower of tiny, spiked horse chestnuts from the big tree by the gate.

At last they finished. They stood back and looked at their work. The little wooden house looked sturdy. Hannah stretched chicken-wire across the front and Helen tacked it into place. There was a light, daytime section and a dark space for the rabbits to sleep in. The hutch needed a lining of straw, then it would be ready for Sugar and Spice to live in.

'I'll fetch the straw!' Helen cried, pleased with their efforts. Speckle yapped and ran with her into the barn. Since the time when the twins had rescued him from the old quarry, he went everywhere with them. They were proud of the way he'd learnt to follow orders. One day, they hoped, Speckle would become a real farm dog, learning how to round up sheep.

'I'll bring the rabbits.' Hannah followed.

David Moore lifted the finished hutch on to a stone ledge under the chestnut tree. Hannah carried the box from the barn. Carefully she lifted little Sugar out of the box. The rabbit snuggled soft and white in the palm of her hand. Her ears and nose twitched, her pink eyes darted here and there.

Meanwhile, Helen lifted Spice and showed her the hutch. The second rabbit, the one with flecks of brown on her back, sniffed at the clean straw. She hopped from Helen's hand into her new home. 'She likes it!' Helen smiled and watched Spice bob towards the dish of dried food they'd bought specially.

Hannah put Sugar into the hutch, then closed the

door. 'So does Sugar, look!' The rabbit sat combing her whiskers with her front paws.

Their dad rubbed his curly brown hair. 'I should think so too! This is a luxury home, remember!' He packed away his tools and put them in their small stone shed. Then he glanced over the wall and down their lane. 'Here comes your mother now. I'll go and put the kettle on for a cup of tea.'

He left them to admire their handiwork as Mary Moore drove into the yard.

'Guess what,' their mum began. She sat with her feet up, sipping the hot tea their dad had made. The twins were at the kitchen table reading all about rabbits in their pets book. 'I bumped into Barbara Wesley when I called in at Luke's shop on my way home.' Miss Wesley taught at Doveton Junior, where the twins went to school.

'And?' David Moore fixed a new film into his camera. He was a photographer when he wasn't busy mending and building things at Home Farm.

'She's going on holiday for a few days.' Mary Moore took another sip of tea. She'd changed out of her cafe clothes into a pair of jeans and a bright blue T-shirt, and she'd fastened her long dark hair into a loose ponytail.

'And?' their dad said again.

Helen and Hannah weren't really listening. Speckle had his front paws on the table, watching what they were up to. The clock ticked in the hallway, there was peace and quiet out on the fell as the sun went down and the new baby rabbits nestled in the straw in their new hutch in the farmyard.

'As a matter of fact, she asked me if we'd look after Sinbad for her while she's away.'

Still the twins took no notice. To Helen and Hannah, the name "Miss Wesley" meant school. They'd just broken up for the summer holidays. Why think about Miss Wesley when there were six weeks of freedom ahead?

'Who's Sinbad?' David Moore flicked little levers and clicked his camera shut. He pointed it at Speckle and took a quick shot.

'Her cat.'

Hannah and Helen's ears suddenly pricked up.

'What did you say to her?' their dad asked.

The twins thought they knew the answer: no. Their mum would have said they had enough on their plates with Speckle and the geese and the hens, and now Sugar and Spice.

Mary Moore pursed her lips and pulled a face. 'Barbara said Sinbad *hates* being left by himself. She said a neighbour could go in to feed him for the three days, but he'd be miserable at home alone. So she wondered if we would have him to stay.' There was another long pause.

'Come on, Mum, what did *you* say?' Helen insisted.

'I said yes!' she confessed.

The twins jumped up open-mouthed.

'Well, it's only for three days,' she pointed out. She got to her feet and headed for the door, flower-cutters in hand. She was on her way out to cut pink roses that grew up the side of the house. 'Sinbad's a little sweetie. I don't expect he'll be any trouble.'

Helen stared at Hannah. 'She said yes! We can actually look after Miss Wesley's cat!'

'What did she say his name was?' Hannah hugged herself with excitement.

'Sinbad.'

'The pirate,' their dad chipped in. He looked as surprised as the twins. 'I wonder what came over your mother?'

'It's only one little cat,' Hannah pointed out. 'He's hardly going to be a problem, is he?'

'Cats are easy,' Helen agreed. She tempted Speckle with the core from the apple she was eating. Speckle sat, the picture of patience, waiting for the apple core to drop. 'Cats can look after themselves.'

Hannah nodded. 'You don't have to take them for walks or anything. Anyway Mum's in a good mood because it's Dad's birthday soon. I expect that's why she said yes.'

'When did Miss Wesley say she'd bring Sinbad?' Helen asked.

Their mum had come back into the house with an armful of pink flowers. She was humming happily.

'Now. I just heard the car coming up the lane.' She lifted a glass vase from the dresser and filled it with water.

Helen and Hannah didn't wait to hear more. They ran outside to wait for the teacher's car.

'We're going to be cat-sitters!' Hannah cried. She could still hardly believe it.

Miss Wesley arrived at last. She parked in the farmyard, then lifted a cat basket from the car. The twins went to meet Sinbad.

The teacher put the wicker basket on the ground. She lifted the lid. 'What do you think?'

Out popped a fluffy black head. A pair of bright green eyes flashed up at them. The cat looked around the farmyard and purred at the hens. Then, slowly, stretching and arching his back, he stepped on to firm ground.

'He's beautiful!' Helen gasped.

'He's jet black,' Hannah sighed.

'Look at his white whiskers!'

'And his green eyes!'

A pink tongue appeared. 'Miaow!' Sinbad said hello.

The twins were speechless with delight. They thought their visitor was too wonderful for words. Even Speckle stopped in his tracks as Sinbad picked his way towards the house, tail up, high-stepping between their legs, as if he knew he was the guest of honour.

'Show off!' Miss Wesley laughed at him. She turned to chat with their mum.

'He's checking us out to see if we're good enough!' Helen watched the cat peer inside their cosy kitchen. He headed straight for a soft chair piled high with cushions.

Only the best for him! Hannah thought as he jumped up on to the chair and sat like a proud foreign prince.

'Do you think he likes us?'

Slowly the twins followed him inside. Sinbad purred from the pile of crimson cushions.

'It looks like he's decided to stay, at any rate.' Hannah took hold of Speckle's collar and took him to say hello. Even the dog seemed to be shy. He rested his chin on the seat of the chair and wagged his tail gently.

Sinbad swiped a lazy paw at him and yawned.

The twins turned and smiled, as Miss Wesley and their mum appeared in the doorway.

'Well, what do you think?' Mary Moore asked.

'He's gorgeous!' the twins said in one breath.

'So you think you'll enjoy cat-sitting?' The teacher came in and stroked Sinbad's coal-black fur.

'It'll be brilliant!'

'It'll be fantastic!'

The black cat seemed to cast a spell over them both. They'd fallen head over heels in love with him.

'Well,' Miss Wesley said. 'Be warned. He can sometimes be a bit of a handful!'

'On no!' Hannah and Helen protested.

'Hear that, Sinbad?' Miss Wesley smiled. 'They don't believe you can be bad!'

'He'll be fine,' their mum said. She showed Miss Wesley to the door. 'Don't worry about Sinbad. The girls are crazy about animals, he'll be very well looked after.'

'Spoilt to death, you mean,' their dad joked.

Their voices faded into the background. Helen and Hannah stayed in the kitchen with Speckle and Sinbad.

From the chair Sinbad purred. He made himself at home, knowing that Helen and Hannah were already his slaves. He seemed to smile as he settled down to sleep. In the background, they heard the teacher's car drive off.

The twins gazed at the cat.

'Three whole days!' Helen whispered. 'We've got him for three whole days!'

Two

'Cats are easy. They look after themselves! Now, where did I hear that?' David Moore watched the twins trying to coax Sinbad to eat his breakfast.

Dishes of cat food, boiled fish and chicken scraps lay scattered around the kitchen floor. Sinbad would have none of them. Helen tried him with a bowl of mashed sardines. Sinbad sniffed and turned up his nose.

'He *is* a fussy eater,' Hannah admitted.

'Fussy!' Their dad echoed, then raised his eyebrows.

Helen crawled after the fluffy black cat. 'Here, Sinbad, here's a nice dish of yummy salmon!' Open cans littered the table. They'd tried just about everything they could think of.

Sinbad scorned the salmon. With a twitch of his tail, he swerved past Helen out of the door. He'd spotted the hens in the farmyard. Soon he crouched and pounced, setting up a dreadful cackle. The hens squawked and flapped out of Sinbad's way.

'Oh no you don't!' Hannah ran after him. She caught one of the hens in both arms.

The cat crouched at her feet. Then, in a flash, he turned tail and chose another plump brown hen to chase. They scattered, flapping on to the wall and clucking furiously. Sinbad leapt easily after them. Then he spied Lucy and Dandy in the next field. The geese hissed and spread their wings.

'Sinbad, no!' Helen warned. She used her sternest voice.

The cat stared at the geese. They were twice his size. He decided to back off, and went to choose a sunny spot to rest instead. He lay down on top of the wall next to the new rabbit hutch. Inside, Sugar and Spice scuffled nervously in their straw beds.

'Phew!' Helen and Hannah had watched his antics

in dismay. All this fuss, just to get Sinbad to eat his breakfast.

'What if he refuses to eat and he starves to death before Miss Wesley comes back?' Hannah asked. She was worried. Despite their best efforts, he hadn't eaten a thing.

'Oh, he won't.' Helen tried to steady her voice. She was worried too; about what their mum would say when she came back and saw all the open, unused tins lying about in the kitchen. 'He'll eat when he's hungry.' She glanced down at Speckle, who sat quietly through all the fuss. 'Let's feed everyone else, and just hope Sinbad settles down.'

So they got on with their morning chores while the cat lazed in the sun. Helen gave Speckle his breakfast of dried food, Hannah scattered grain for the hens. The baby rabbits came out of their nest to nibble nervously at lettuce leaves which Helen had pushed through the wire of their hutch. Sinbad only blinked and soaked up the sun.

They turned their backs for a second to tend to the grey geese. Helen poured fresh water into their metal bath, Hannah dropped pellets of food on the scratched earth. When they looked again, Sinbad had vanished.

'Sinbad!' Helen sounded cross.

'Here, Sinbad!' Hannah put on a high, sweet voice to tempt him back.

'Come on, we'd better find out what he's up to!' Helen climbed the wall and stomped across the yard.

They searched and searched. Eventually, they found him in the barn, his nose deep into Speckle's breakfast. He munched the dry biscuits while the poor dog looked on.

'You bad cat!' Helen flapped her arms at him, and the chase began again.

Sinbad gave a mighty leap on to a ladder leading to the hayloft. The twins scrambled after him, in time to see him jump from a narrow window onto a sloping roof. He shot across the slates and down amongst the branches of the rose tree that grew up the side of the house. He dropped to the ground like a black shadow, slunk across the yard, stalking hens as he went.

'Wow!' Hannah pushed her hair from her face. They hurried down the ladder and out into the yard, in time to see Sinbad, bored now with the clumsy hens, fixing his glittering green eyes on a blackbird's nest. He sat still as stone, staring into the leafy branches of the horse chestnut tree, awaiting his chance.

'Oh!' Hannah gasped, out of breath.

'Sinbad, no!' Helen used her war-cry to shoo him away.

The blackbirds hidden in the tree set up a shrill warning. The cat flicked his tail at Hannah and stole off.

She flopped against the wall. 'Did I say cats were easy?'

'I'm tired out!' Helen complained. She kept a wary eye on Sinbad.

'I suppose it's just the way they're made,' Hannah said. 'They're meant to stalk and hunt and everything, aren't they?' She tried to make excuses.

'Yes but, at this rate we won't last the three days!'

'He's not done any real harm, though, has he?'

'So far!' Helen watched Sinbad choose another sunny spot. He sat, licked his paws and cleaned behind his pointed black ears.

'See, he's sweet!' Hannah forgave him on the spot. She turned to faithful Speckle and patted his head. 'You'll keep an eye on him for us, won't you, boy?'

The dog settled by the wall, not far from Sinbad.

Soon it seemed safe for the twins to go inside.

'How's it going?' David Moore called down from his attic dark-room. He was working on a big job for a wildlife magazine, printing pictures of foxes at night.

'Fine!' Hannah called back.

'Sort of,' Helen added. 'But to tell you the truth, I'd rather come out with you in the dead of night to photograph foxes and badgers. It's less of a strain than cat-sitting!'

'Good.' Her absent-minded dad hadn't really heard. 'Well, keep an eye on him,' he warned. 'We don't want him wandering off.'

Famous last words. After five minutes, the twins heard a loud bark from Speckle.

'Uh-oh!' Helen nipped out to check on Sinbad. She found Speckle standing on his hind legs, front paws resting on the gate. He barked, but there was no sign of the cat in his sunny spot by the wall.

'Sinbad, where have you got to now?' Helen cried. She looked up and down the empty lane.

'What's up? Where's he gone?' Hannah joined her at the gate.

'If I knew that, I wouldn't be standing here like an idiot yelling his name, would I?'

Hannah shrugged. 'Keep your hair on. Sinbad, here!'

But cats aren't like dogs, who come when you call. 'Looks like he's gone walkabout,' Helen sighed.

'Down into the village?' Hannah wondered.

'Or up on to the fell? Now I bet we have to spend the whole day looking for him.' Helen was cross. 'He may look like a little angel, with his fluffy black fur and his wide green eyes. But really he's a little . . . devil!'

The twins set out after him, hearts in their mouths, wondering what he would get up to next.

Three

'Sinbad, here, puss, puss, puss!'

'Where on earth are you, you bad cat?'

Hannah and Helen looked everywhere. They set Speckle on his trail and scouted down the lane, past Fred Hunt's ginger tom at the gate of High Hartwell, past old Ben the sheepdog at Lakeside Farm. Ben's owner, John Fox, promised to keep a lookout for Sinbad.

'You say it's the teacher's cat?' He lifted his cap and scratched his forehead. 'I never knew Mr Winter had a cat.'

Mr Winter was the strict old man who used to run

the village school. The twins had learned to stay away from him and his sharp tongue. 'No, not him,' Helen told John. 'The young teacher, Miss Wesley. It's her cat we're looking after.'

He nodded. 'In that case, I'll definitely keep an eye open.' He winked. 'I wouldn't want that nice young lass to be worried about a missing pet!'

They thanked him and ran on, frittering away a lovely sunny day looking for the runaway.

'Sinbad, here, puss!' They went on calling. Their cries echoed down every nook and cranny of the pretty village.

There was no sign of him down by the lake. The lady in the ice-cream cafe shook her head. No sign in the main street either. Luke Martin came out on to the doorstep of his shop. His flock of white doves cooed gently from their wooden house high on the wall.

'No, I'd soon know if a stray cat came calling.' He nodded at the birds. 'What's that saying about setting the cat among the pigeons? There'd be an almighty row if Sinbad paid us a visit!'

The twins agreed. Sinbad hadn't come this way, then. Leg-weary, they spent the morning searching in the village. In the afternoon, they climbed the rocky slopes above Home Farm. But Sinbad hadn't come this way either.

'What now?' Hannah bent to pat Speckle. The poor dog hadn't been able to pick up the cat's trail. He sat quiet at her side.

'I'm hungry!' Helen heard her stomach rumble. 'Or was that you?'

'No, you!'

'Or Speckle!' It was Helen's turn to give him a friendly pat. His tail wagged. 'Good boy. You're hungry too, aren't you?'

Hannah looked at her watch. 'I suppose it *is* teatime.' She took one last look up the steep hillside. 'I hate to give up before we find him, though.'

'Oh, come on!' Helen decided. 'Either he'll come home by himself, or we'll have to come back out after tea.' She led the way back to Home Farm.

'This is really great!' Hannah muttered.

'What is?'

'We lose Sinbad on his very first day at Home Farm!'

'He lost himself.'

But Hannah stopped. They'd reached the end of their lane and the house was in sight. 'No, we lost him. A cat can't be expected to know he can't just wander off. We should've kept an eye on him.'

'Well, we will when we find him,' Helen promised. She ran ahead.

'If!' Hannah put her right. 'If we find him.'

'Sinbad!' the twins cried in one breath.

They found the cat sitting large as life on the red cushions of his favourite kitchen chair. He looked as if butter wouldn't melt in his mouth.

'There you are!' Helen scolded. 'Where have you been? We've been looking everywhere!'

'Sinbad, you're safe!' Hannah flopped into

another chair. Then she heard their mum's car drive through the gate. She jumped up again. 'Quick, let's clear up!'

They whisked the dishes and cans out of sight. By the time their mum came into the kitchen, the room was tidy, and Sinbad sat looking serene.

But Mary Moore was serious. She put her bag on the table and sank into a chair. Their dad came down from his dark-room to ask about her day.

'Busy,' she sighed. 'A whole bus-load came into the cafe for lunch.' Her little health food cafe was popular with Nesfield tourists.

'Well, it's good for business, anyway.' David Moore spread his new photographs on the table. 'What do you think?'

The pictures were sharp and clear. You could see every detail on the foxes' clever faces; the pointed ears and bright eyes.

'Brilliant!' The twins loved to look at his work.

'Very good,' their mum agreed. She turned to Hannah and Helen. 'How did Sinbad behave himself?'

Hannah swallowed hard. 'OK,' she said faintly.

'Well, actually . . .' Helen felt herself go red. 'He went missing for a bit. We had to go looking for him.'

'I thought so.' Their mum glanced at the purring cat.

'Why, what's wrong?' David Moore went to put the kettle on as usual.

'I stopped in at Luke's. There's been some trouble in the village this afternoon.'

The twins froze, dreading what was coming next. This was something about Sinbad, they felt sure.

Mary Moore went on. 'No one is sure who's to blame, but Luke told me that something or someone had got in amongst his doves. It was just before he shut up shop for the day. There was a heck of a racket outside, and he went to investigate, but he got there too late to catch the culprit. There were white feathers flying and all the birds were squawking like mad. He couldn't think what had got into them!'

Helen pictured the frenzy of gentle white doves. 'Does he say it was definitely Sinbad?' she asked with a frown.

'Wait, that's not all. A little bit earlier, Mr Winter came into the shop in a terrible temper. Apparently, his little dog had run yapping into the garden to chase off some intruder. He came back in with a bad scratch on his nose. Mr Winter had to take him to the vet.

Luke let it slip that you'd been in looking for a runaway cat.'

'Sinbad wouldn't attack a dog!' Hannah protested.

'He's only a harmless little cat,' Helen agreed.

'Well, someone or something has been causing trouble.' Mrs Moore stared long and hard at their guest.

'Not Sinbad!' the twins cried. Sinbad purred.

'Oh, butter wouldn't melt, would it?' Their dad laughed. 'What if it turns out he's the cat from hell!'

The twins looked glum.

'Well,' their mum decided at last. They all stared at Sinbad on his rich red cushions. 'We'll just have to keep a better eye on him, that's all. As Barbara said, he can be a bit of a handful!'

But the twins were convinced, in spite of everything, that Sinbad couldn't possibly be so naughty. They stole off to their bedroom to talk things through.

'Listen, he did stalk the hens and steal Speckle's breakfast,' Helen admitted.

'And he did run off for the day,' Hannah said slowly. 'But I don't believe he terrified Luke's doves or took a chunk out of Puppy's nose.'

'So how do we prove it?'

Hannah shook her head. 'That's the problem. If Mr Winter puts the blame on Sinbad, we'll have to do our best to stick up for him.'

Helen led the way downstairs. 'If only cats could talk.'

'Or dogs.' Hannah wished Puppy could have identified his attacker. 'Or doves.'

They went into the kitchen to stroke Sinbad's soft black fur. 'You be a good boy,' Hannah said gently. 'No more wandering off, OK? If you do, you're going to get us into a mess, you hear?'

It was possible that from now on, poor Sinbad would get the blame for every tiny thing that went wrong in the village. Sinbad purred. He loved to be stroked. He spread like a lord on his plump cushions. Then he yawned. In seconds he was fast asleep.

Four

'Mmm, what's that?' Helen woke late on Sunday morning. The smell of baking already wafted up the stairs.

'Dad's birthday cake!' Hannah leapt out of bed. She'd smelt it too. It was their dad's birthday. 'Mum's making something special!' They ran downstairs in their pyjamas to help.

'Can we decorate it?' Helen asked. The smell of the cake baking in the old Aga was delicious.

'Yes, but shh, it's meant to be a secret.' Mary Moore smiled. 'Your dad's going out to play cricket this morning. I thought we'd do the icing while he's out.'

'Where's Sinbad?' Helen saw that his chair was empty. Her heart gave a little lurch.

'Having his breakfast,' her mum said calmly. 'It looks like he's decided to behave himself today.'

They found him under the table. He lapped steadily at a saucer of milk. When he finished the last drop, he padded towards the stairs. Hannah followed him to the top storey, where he chose a sunny window-sill on the landing. There he curled up out of the way.

'He's OK, he's sleeping,' she reported when she went back to the kitchen.

Helen was already busy preparing to ice the cake. Her nose was dusted with icing-sugar. But she threw a tea-towel over everything as she heard her dad come downstairs.

'What's going on?' He poked his head round the door, then came in. He wore his cream sweater with the maroon stripe round its V-neck, and his white cricket trousers.

'Nothing!' they sang out. Then they ran and hugged him Happy Birthday.

He hugged them back, a grin spreading across his sleepy face.

'How old are you?' Helen needed to check the number of candles for the cake.

'Thirty . . . something. Never you mind.' He wrinkled his nose.

'Aah, Dad!'

'Thirty-five,' Hannah slipped in.

'Thanks, Hann!' He pretended to stoop and creak as he headed for the door. 'I'll be drawing my pension next!'

'Have a good game,' Mary called.

'Yes, see you later. Bye, everyone! Bye, Speckle! And remember, look after that cat!'

'Don't worry, he's upstairs asleep,' Hannah told him.

'Good. Just so long as he stays that way!'

Then he was gone, and they spent the rest of the morning working on the birthday cake. It came out of the oven golden-brown, risen in the middle like a little volcano, smelling of sugar and eggs. They let it cool. Helen mixed the sugar-icing and poured it all over the cake. Again they waited. When the icing was set, Hannah took a dish of strawberries from the fridge. She decorated the cake with fruit and squirts of whipped cream. Helen finished it off with candles, arranged in a neat circle. Then they stood back.

'Perfect!' Their mum lifted the cake and took it through to the lounge, where it was nice and cool. The twins watched as she set it on the coffee table by the sofa. 'Keep this door closed,' she warned. Then she went off to wash up the baking things.

The wonderful cake stood on the table in the lounge. Every so often the twins would open the door a crack and peep at it. It sat there, piled high with strawberries and cream, with the proud white candles.

Helen and Hannah sat for ages at the kitchen table making a birthday card. They stuck a close-up photograph of Speckle on the front, and inside there was a rhyme they made up themselves. The morning had passed before they knew it.

'Quick!' Mary Moore spied their dad coming home. The car drove into the yard. 'He's here. Are we ready?'

Helen and Hannah had just wrapped a box of his favourite chocolates in bright red paper. The last piece of sellotape was in place when their dad finally walked into the room.

'Happy Birthday!' They ran to him with the present and card. Speckle, who had been sunning himself in the yard, came to join in the fun.

'Again?' David Moore beamed at the twins. He opened the present and card, then gave them another big hug. 'They're smashing!' He read the card again, then picked up the present.

'Wait here!' Helen told him.

'We've got another surprise,' Hannah explained.

They ran into the lounge to fetch the cake.

But when Helen opened the door, she saw at once what had happened to their dad's beautiful birthday cake. Two strawberries had toppled on to the table and a chunk of cream was missing. There was a perfect paw-print in the sugar-icing. 'Look!' She stared in dismay.

Hannah crept into the room behind her. They'd kept the door shut, thinking that the cake was safe. But as she went in, she spotted a silent black shape leap from the windowsill. Sinbad had climbed through the open window to get at the cake. 'Oh no, Sinbad!'

Helen ran to the window, while Hannah bent over the cake. 'Sinbad!' she echoed through gritted teeth. There he was strutting across the yard, the cat that got the cream!

'It could have been anyone; a stray, or even a . . . a

fox!' Hannah made feeble excuses. She perched the strawberries back on the cake and tried to mend the decoration.

'No, come and look. I can still see him!' This time he'd taken things too far. 'It was Sinbad all right!'

'But how was he to know?' Hannah picked up the cake. 'Anyway, it doesn't look too bad. Maybe Dad won't notice.' She'd worked hard to make the cake look right.

Helen frowned at the paw-print. Then she grinned. 'Trust Sinbad! Let's tell Dad it's a cat's way of saying Happy Birthday!'

Hannah cheered up. 'Yes, and don't mention the cream, OK?' Sinbad had helped himself to the cake, but it wasn't the end of the world. 'Ready?'

She didn't want to spoil her dad's birthday, so Helen agreed to cover up for the pirate cat. 'OK, let's go!'

They sang "Happy Birthday" as they trooped into the kitchen. Mary Moore lit the candles and their dad blew them out with a wish, without even noticing the paw-print. But their mum did. She gave the twins a frown as she cut carefully round it.

'What did you wish, Dad?' Helen cried.

'I can't tell you, or it won't come true.' He took a giant bite out of the slice Hannah gave to him.

'I tell you what I wish,' Mary Moore said, as they went outside to sit in the sun. Sinbad was there first. He blinked sweetly at them from the windowsill.

'What?' Hannah had an idea what this wish would be.

'I wish I could get my hands on that little rascal!' She closed her eyes, sighed, and turned her face towards the sun.

'Only one more day,' their dad reminded her. 'Then he goes home, thank heavens!'

'Mum, Dad, you'll hurt his feelings!' Hannah would stick up for Sinbad until the end.

'Him? He hasn't got any!' David Moore closed his eyes and began to doze.

Soon they all settled down. The grown-ups snoozed, the twins played quietly with Speckle, while Sinbad folded his front paws under him and decided what mischief he could get up to next.

They found out early next morning, soon after their mum had set off for work.

'Hannah-Helen!' Their dad called from his dark-room in the attic. He said their names as if they were one person.

'Uh-oh!' Helen knew this was trouble. It was unheard of for him to sound this angry.

'I bet it's old Sinbad again,' Hannah whispered with a sinking heart. Together they went upstairs.

Their easy-going dad looked like thunder. His face was red, his forehead wrinkled. 'It's that cat. He's hiding in here somewhere. And look what he's done!' Jars of chemicals were tipped on their sides, dishes were spilt, rolls of film lay tangled on the table.

'Are you sure it was him?' Hannah asked the usual question.

David Moore waggled his finger. 'Here's the proof.' He pointed to a dirty wet paw mark on a sheet of white card. 'He's messed up dozens of negatives and spilt stuff all over these new prints. It's my wildlife work, the foxes and badgers. All ruined!' He shrugged helplessly. 'It means I'll have to start again.'

The twins shook their heads sadly. 'We're sorry, Dad, we really are!'

'I'm not angry with you. It's not your fault; it's that cat!'

As if he knew the game was up, Sinbad tried to creep silently from the room. He slunk out from under the bench and stole towards the door.

But David Moore spotted him. 'Oh no you don't!' He slammed the door shut, and in the eerie red safety light of the dark-room he chased the cat from bench to stool, along the work surfaces down on to the floor. At last he cornered him under a chair. The twins stood by. 'Gotcha!' He made a grab for Sinbad and caught him by the scruff of the neck.

'Careful Dad, you'll hurt him!' Hannah warned.

'Hurt him! He'll be lucky if I don't strangle him!'

Her dad marched out of the room. The cat didn't struggle; he knew it was useless.

Helen was the first to recover. She ran after her dad, down the stairs. 'Where are you taking him?' She followed him into the farmyard. The hens by the door scattered as he strode out.

'I'm putting him in the shed until Barbara comes to collect him. And no one is to go near him, understand?'

The twins nodded. Sinbad gave a faint miaow. The shed was the small stone building next to the barn. It was where they kept tools and plant-pots. There were no windows, no light, and no way of escape, even for clever Sinbad.

Hannah grabbed Helen by the arm. 'Poor cat. That's a horrible place to put him.' Dark and smelly, with cobwebs hanging from the roof and oil stains on the floor.

'Yes, but Dad's upset. What can we do?'

They stared miserably as David Moore flung open the shed door. A strong, musty smell drifted out. Sinbad miaowed again, even fainter than before.

Then their dad put the cat into the dark shed and banged the door shut. He turned to the twins. 'Look,

40

I know it's not very nice in there. But at least it will keep him out of mischief until he goes home! And it's not for long.'

They watched him march back to the house. Out in the yard, the hens began to peck once more. Speckle came up quietly and put his head against Helen's leg. His tail was down, he looked sad and upset.

'There, boy, never mind.' Helen comforted him. 'Like Dad says, it's not for long. Sinbad will be OK.'

But it was hard to walk away and just leave him there. They listened carefully. From behind the door they heard a long, loud miaow.

'He's scared stiff,' Hannah said, trembling herself.

Speckle heard too. He lay down close to the shed door, snuffling at the gap and whining.

All alone and frightened, Sinbad called for help.

Five

'And one more thing!' Mr Winter wagged his finger at the twins. 'If your family agrees in future to look after someone else's cat or dog, please make quite sure that you know what you're doing!'

It was Monday lunch-time. Mr Winter had driven up to Home Farm to tell them off. He'd put word round Doveton that Sinbad was the latest village pest. Now he was on the warpath.

Helen and Hannah were lost for words. Luckily, Sinbad was still locked safely inside the shed. Puppy sat in the back seat, a dab of white ointment on his nose. Their dad stood, arms folded, by the kitchen door, while Mr Winter, dressed in his navy blue blazer, stood to attention, shoulders back, chest out, and went on and on.

'You admit that the cat gave you the slip on Saturday?' He poked his face at Helen, demanding an answer.

Helen nodded. 'Yes, but we're not sure he went down to Doveton. No one actually saw him.'

'You can't accuse someone without proof,' Hannah appealed to her dad. The twins stuck by their promise to defend Sinbad.

Helen nodded extra hard.

'Hmph.' Mr Winter turned to her. 'And you admit that he's totally out of control?'

Hannah took a deep breath. 'Yes, but you can't train a cat to do as he's told. Not like Speckle, for instance.'

By the shed door, Speckle's head went up. His tail wagged at the mention of his name.

'All the more reason to put this cat where you can keep an eye on him, instead of letting him sneak off to attack other people's pets!' Mr Winter knitted his bushy eyebrows. His forehead was criss-crossed with frown-lines.

Helen bit her lip. She could think of lots she wanted

to say, but she knew better than to argue back. Anyway, Mr Winter was an expert at telling kids off, she realised. Better to let him get it out of his system. She sneaked a look at Hannah, as the ex-school-teacher rattled on.

'I had to take poor Puppy to the vet after his encounter with that vicious cat! His nose was cut to ribbons!' He turned to the only other sensible person on the scene; David Moore. 'I do hate to see an animal in pain, don't you!'

'Of course,' he said quietly. His grey eyes had lost all their smile and bounce.

'The treatment cost me twenty-five pounds!' Mr Winter stared him in the face.

The twins watched their dad fish into his pocket. 'In that case, you must let me pay the vet's fee,' he insisted. He handed over the notes without fuss.

'Oh no!' Mr Winter pretended to push them away.

'Yes, please!'

'Oh, very well.' He took them and tucked them carefully into his breast pocket. Then he turned back to Helen and Hannah. 'Now you see what carelessness costs!'

They wished they could switch Mr Winter off, like

a television set. From the back seat of the car, Puppy jumped up at the window and barked. From inside the shed, Sinbad gave a faint miaow. Luckily, the dog drowned out the sound.

'Yes, yes, I'm coming, Puppy!' Mr Winter glanced round the farmyard. 'You still have a lot to do, I see,' he said to David Moore. He meant the gate, still broken, the grass poking up through the flagstones, the rattling doors and windows. He wandered here and there, peering nosily through the kitchen door.

Their dad smiled stiffly. 'It's coming on slowly.'

'Hmm.' The old teacher awarded marks for effort; six out of ten. He smiled in what he thought was a kind way. 'It's a brave thing to take on a place like this.'

Then his ears pricked up. He leaned his head towards the shed. 'Did I hear a cat?' he asked. Immediately, his face creased into its old frown.

Helen and Hannah sagged. 'You'd think Sinbad would have the sense to keep quiet!' Helen whispered without moving her lips. But no; he began to wail and cry out. They watched as Mr Winter was drawn towards the sound.

'Yes, it's a cat. Can you hear it?' He put his ear close

to the shed door. 'It's *the* cat, isn't it?'

The twins nodded.

'We're keeping him safe in there until Barbara Wesley comes back to collect him,' their dad said.

There was a glint in the old schoolteacher's eye. 'I should think so too!' He checked the shed. 'Nice and secure! I take it this means he isn't safe to be let loose?'

'Miaow!' Sinbad let his feelings be known. He'd heard the voices close to his prison door.

Hannah closed her eyes. Poor Sinbad! Her soft heart melted.

'Yes, he's better off in there.' Their dad wanted to get on with his work. 'I'm sorry Sinbad got into a fight with Puppy,' he told Mr Winter. 'And I'm sorry you had the trouble of having to go to the vet. It won't happen again.' He checked the latch on the shed door. It was firmly shut.

'Very good.' Mr Winter gave a short nod.

'Now, if you'll excuse me, I have some work to catch up on.' David Moore made for the house.

'Quite. And I can go and tell Mr Martin that his doves are safe.' In turn, Mr Winter headed for his car. 'Just so long as that cat stays locked up!' He gave the twins a warning look, then got into his car and started the engine. Puppy yapped and yapped as he drove away from Home Farm.

'Ouch!' their dad said quietly. But he was too busy to stay and talk. 'See you later,' he told Helen and Hannah. He took the stairs to the attic two at a time.

'Look, he's been in there, in the dark, all alone for hours and hours!' Hannah whispered to Helen. She carried a newspaper and a red cushion under one arm. All afternoon she'd listened to Sinbad miaowing from behind the shed door.

Helen watched her take the cushion outside. 'Yes, but cats don't mind the dark,' she reminded her.

'Shh!' Hannah warned. Their dad was still upstairs, hard at work. Softly she crept across the yard to the shed. 'That doesn't mean to say that Sinbad can't be nice and comfy in there.'

Helen ran after her. She wasn't sure they were doing the right thing. After all, their dad had said not to go anywhere near Sinbad. 'But it's only for a few more hours. Miss Wesley will be back later this evening!'

Hannah stuck out her chin. 'I want to take him his favourite cushion, that's all!'

Sinbad's miaows grew louder. Helen gave in. 'Oh, OK, wait for me!' She glanced up at the attic window. It was shut tight and covered in black material for their dad's photography work. No one could see what they were up to. 'Wait, wait!' She made sure that the hens were out of harm's way. If Sinbad spotted them when they opened the shed door, it could be chaos.

Hannah waited while Helen shooed the hens into the field with Lucy and Dandy. They clucked and complained as they went. 'Shh!' she warned again.

When Helen came back, her brown eyes were lit up with excitement. 'Are you sure about this?' You don't think it's a bit risky?'

Hannah shook her head. 'I just feel sorry for him, that's all. Ready?'

'Wait!' Helen called Speckle to keep a lookout. 'Here, boy! Yep, ready! I'll lift the latch, OK? When the door's open a crack, you nip in with the cushion!'

Hannah's plan was to line the shed floor with the newspaper and put the cushion on top. Then at least Sinbad would be able to have a cosy nap until Miss Wesley came. 'OK!' She got ready to dart inside.

'I wish Sinbad would pipe down!' Helen had one hand on the iron latch. She clicked it up. Sinbad howled.

'Shh, Sinbad!' Hannah clutched the cushion. She nodded again at Helen.

Helen opened the door a chink. A crack of sunlight shot across the floor of the dark shed. She peered inside. All she could see were the cat's bright green eyes gleaming in the far corner. 'He's over there!' she whispered. 'When I open the door a bit more, you have to get in there quick, so I can shut it again, OK?'

Hannah got ready. The door opened and she slipped safely inside. It clicked shut behind her. The shed was pitch-dark.

Sinbad's eyes stared. He stopped howling and looked suspiciously at her. Gradually her eyes grew used to the dark; she could make out the rough old walls, a pile of clay plant-pots, a bag of tools. So she got to work, lining the floor with paper. She felt Sinbad rub against her legs.

'You OK in there?' Helen whispered through the cracks in the door.

'Fine. He's pleased to see me!' Hannah put the cushion on the newspaper, nice and comfy.

'Get a move on, then,' Helen urged.

Hannah picked Sinbad up and showed him his

new bed. 'This is for you,' she explained. 'Now, stay here until it's time to go home.'

He seemed to understand. Obediently he sat on the velvety cushion. He purred and blinked up at her.

'Great! Good boy!' Hannah stared down at him, her eyes fuzzy in the dark. She tapped on the door.

'Ready?' Helen whispered.

'Yep. He's settled down. I can come out now.' She got ready to make a quick exit.

Helen eased the door open. The streak of light shot across the floor. Suddenly, Sinbad leapt to his feet. He cleared the plant-pots and the toolbox and was clean out of the door.

'Sinbad, no!' Hannah cried, too late.

Outside, Helen caught sight of a black streak. He shot out of the narrow opening. One leap and he was free. Speckle barked, Hannah cried out. Sinbad got clean away.

The twins watched as he streaked out of the gate, down the lane. Disaster! Sinbad was too clever for them. Now, if he headed for Doveton, Mr Winter and the whole village would be after him.

'Come on, we've got to save him,' Helen said.

'And find out while we're at it who did attack

Puppy and the doves.' Hannah thought quickly as they raced to the gate.

'Yes, we'll clear Sinbad's name!' she vowed.

They were twins with a mission; to save Sinbad and prove to the village that the runaway cat was innocent.

Six

'Speckle, here, boy!' Helen was the first to come to her senses. She called the dog to heel.

'We can't say for sure, but I bet Sinbad headed downhill!' Hannah grabbed Speckle's lead from the gatepost. 'Come on, let's go!'

They left two puzzled geese in the yard and a row of curious hens perched on the wall, staring after them. The race was on!

'This way!' Hannah cried.

They cut through Fred Hunt's farmyard at High Hartwell. The farmer poked his head over a stable door. 'Hey, you'll work up a sweat if you go on like that!' he called. 'And it's only Monday!'

Helen explained they'd no time for jokes. 'Did you see a black cat? We want to know which way he was heading.' Speckle scouted on, nose to the ground.

'Lucky black cat, eh?' The sturdy farmer scratched his head. The chestnut mare in the stable nudged him to one side. She blew noisily down her nostrils and craned her neck to see what was going on.

'*Un*lucky!' Helen told him. 'He escaped from our shed. He's not even ours!'

'Bad luck,' Fred agreed. He had a broad smile on his tanned face. 'It's not the same one as got loose the other day by any chance?'

It seemed everyone had heard about the business with Luke's doves and Mr Winter's dog. 'Yes,' Hannah nodded. 'Did you see him, Mr Hunt? We've got to find him!' She was breathless, her damp hair stuck to her forehead and neck.

The farmer was an unflappable type. He looked hard at the twins. 'I reckon you'll be in more trouble if you don't,' he said slowly. The mare snickered and nodded her head.

'Mr Hunt, could you please tell us which way Sinbad went?' Helen pleaded. People in Doveton never seemed to rush. While they stood and talked, Sinbad would be streaking ahead.

'It's OK, Helen. Speckle's found the trail, look!' Hannah pulled at her sister's arm. Speckle sniffed hard at a stile that led out of Mr Hunt's yard down a footpath to the village.

The farmer nodded. 'Aye, that's it, that's the way he went. Going like the clappers, he was, took the stile in one go. There was no stopping him.'

'Thanks!' Helen and Hannah ran on, hot on the trail.

'Good luck!' Fred Hunt's pleasant voice called after them. 'I say, that's a handy little dog you've got there!'

The twins' heads went up. 'Thanks a lot!' they called again. They were proud of their dog.

'That's it, Speckle, show us where Sinbad went!' Helen encouraged him. He ran with his nose to the ground, down the path, between tall grass and foxgloves, until at last they came to the first house in the village.

'Stop!' Hannah needed a rest. She watched as Speckle paused to sniff this way and that. 'Where's Sinbad? Where is he, boy?'

The dog sniffed at a bench by the roadside and in and out of a nearby bus shelter. He read the ground, nosing everywhere. The trail led him twice round a huge sycamore tree, across the road towards two tall stone gateposts and the double iron gates of Doveton Manor. Then Speckle looked up at them and barked. He sat, and barked again.

'Uh-oh!' Helen saw what he meant. They followed him across the road. 'Oh no, Sinbad's not in there, is he?' She pressed her face to the iron bars and peered through the gate.

The smooth lawns of the manor house rolled on forever. Oak trees lined a curved drive, and at the end of the drive stood a splendid stone house. The house had many big windows, and glass doors leading on to rose-filled patios. There was a gardener at work watering pots of bright flowers that lined the walls.

'Oh no!' Hannah felt weak at the knees. 'Trust Sinbad to trespass on the poshest house in the village.' Doveton Manor belonged to Mr and Mrs Saunders, the richest people around by far.

'Speckle, are you sure?' Helen crouched to the dog's level. He wagged his tail and stared straight down the drive towards the house.

'What do we do now?' Hannah asked. Two kids and

a dog hanging around outside the grand gates would soon attract attention.

'Make a quick getaway?' Helen suggested.

'No, seriously!'

'I am serious! No, I'm not. Sinbad will need all the help he can get if he's gone in there.'

Hannah screwed her mouth tight. She remembered the newspaper and the cushion in the shed at home; telltale signs that they'd been trying to make Sinbad's life more comfortable when he seized his chance to escape. 'We'll be in trouble at Home Farm too,' she said slowly.

Helen scanned the huge green lawns for any sign of the runaway. 'We could always go up to the house and ask!' The gardener had finished watering the flowers and had begun to clip the dead roses off the bushes. They watched from a safe distance.

'OK,' Hannah decided. It was worth it to get Sinbad out of trouble.

'Are you nuts?' Helen nearly choked. 'I was joking again!' The manor house put her off. People who lived in this sort of place looked down their noses and called the police if you were a nuisance. She would rather climb down into a quarry to rescue a dog any day, like they'd done for Speckle. She put one arm round his neck and stared with him through the bars.

Hannah went ahead and tried the gate. 'It's locked,' she said with a frown.

'Good!' Helen got ready to beat a hasty retreat.

'No, it's OK, the gardener's seen us!'

'Oh no!'

'Come on, Helen. If Sinbad is in there, the sooner we get him out the better.'

They stood and watched as the young man put down his tools and headed down the drive towards the gate. Helen backed off, but Hannah stood firm.

'Hello, there.' He put his head to one side and looked at them each in turn. 'You must be the twins from Home Farm.' He was fair-haired and slim, with ears that stuck out slightly. He wore jeans and a faded blue T-shirt.

Hannah nodded.

'Thought so. How can I help?'

Hannah cleared her throat. 'We're looking for a runaway cat.'

'And you think he came this way?'

They nodded. 'He's nice!' Helen whispered as he glanced over his shoulder at the house.

'I can't see any sign of him.' The gardener looked them up and down. 'Still, there's no harm in you coming in for a proper look.'

'Thanks!' Hannah heaved a sigh of relief.

He began to unbolt the gate. 'Keep that dog on a lead, will you? Mr Saunders goes mad if anyone treads on his lawn.'

Helen put Speckle on the lead and the twins stepped through the gates. They clanged shut behind them, then they began to walk slowly up the drive.

The young man sauntered beside them. 'My name's Mark, by the way.'

'I'm Hannah.'

'And I'm Helen.'

'And this is Speckle.'

The house loomed nearer.

'What colour is this cat?' Mark kept his eyes peeled.

'Jet black. Long, fluffy hair, green eyes.' Helen took care to keep to the path.

'Black, you say?' Mark thought carefully as he led them up some broad stone steps on to the rose terrace. There were grey stone statues of women draped in long robes, and naked little boys with wings, all arranged round a pond where white lilies floated, goldfish swam, and a gentle fountain played.

Helen nodded. 'That's right. His trail led here.'

'Hang on a minute. I'll go and ask Mrs Saunders.' He disappeared round the side of the enormous house.

The twins stood and waited. Speckle sat to attention between them, head up, ears pricked.

Helen tried not to picture what Sinbad might have got up to, here among the perfect rose beds and silent statues. Not that he was a bad cat, as people thought, but he was certainly mischievous. She took a peek through some open french doors at a big room full of dark, polished furniture. From inside, she picked up a low sound. It came from a fat green leather armchair, its back towards the window. 'Did you hear that?' She crept closer to the open doors.

'No, what?' Hannah peered over her shoulder. Then she heard it; a low, gentle purring sound coming from the depths of the green chair.

'Sinbad?' Helen whispered. She glanced round. There was no sign of Mark. It was time to act, she decided. 'Here, Hann, you hold Speckle; I'm going in!'

The purring seemed to grow louder. 'Trust him!' Hannah knew that Sinbad loved a touch of luxury. Even from this distance, the chair looked the perfect spot for him to curl up and cat-nap in. She took Speckle's lead and held her breath.

Helen took one last look round the terrace and stepped into the glossy room.

Then, just as Helen vanished from sight, footsteps approached. Two pairs. First came Mark. Hannah gasped. Mark paused and waited. Then a lady joined him. She listened quietly, then when she spoke it was in a low voice. She was tall and slim with neat blonde hair. When she spotted Hannah, she came immediately towards her.

Hannah coughed. Would Helen take the hint? What should she do? She knew that the lady was Mrs Saunders herself. She'd seen her once before, serving behind a stall at the jumble sale in the village hall. Close to, Hannah had time to admire her long fingers and large, grey eyes. She tried to smile and look as if nothing was wrong. Helen, stay where you are! she prayed. Perhaps she could lead Mrs Saunders away from the french doors and give Helen time to grab Sinbad and make her escape.

'Hello, you must be Hannah, or is it Helen?' Mrs Saunders came forward with a smile. 'Mark tells me you've lost your cat?'

Hannah nodded. 'Yes. Well, no! Well, yes, actually! That is, it's not our cat! But yes, we have lost a cat!' She moved her head furiously up and down, and from side to side.

'A black cat?' Mrs Saunders looked puzzled. But she went on smiling kindly at Hannah. 'Now, I think I did see a sweet little black cat earlier on. He was creeping over the lawn, no doubt up to no good!' She laughed. 'I saw him through my kitchen window, but it must have been ten minutes ago, I'm afraid.'

Hannah kept on nodding like mad. *Helen, where are you?* When she spoke up, her voice sounded odd and breathless. 'Could you tell me which way he went, please?' She led Speckle away from the doors towards the steps that went down to the lawn. She pretended to look for the track Sinbad had taken.

Mrs Saunders couldn't have been nicer. 'Let me see. I think he was making for the terrace here, towards our pond. I mentioned it to Geoffrey and he came out to shoo him off. Because of the fish, you see!' She explained to Hannah. 'That's the last we saw of him, I'm afraid.'

'So you don't know where he went next?' Hannah was running out of questions. If Mrs Saunders did but know it, Sinbad had doubled back to take a nap in one of her best leather chairs! *Come on, Helen!* she said to herself. *What on earth is keeping you?*

Inside the house, Helen steadied her nerves and tiptoed towards the green chair. The cat hidden in its depths was purring like an engine; purr-purr, purr-purr-purrr!

She went down on all fours on to the smooth, polished floor. She would take Sinbad by surprise and creep up on him from behind without making a sound. She would pounce and take him prisoner.

Outside she could hear a woman's voice. Her heart

thumped. She only hoped that Hannah could side-track the owner of the voice long enough for her to catch the pirate cat. Slowly she inched forward.

A floorboard creaked. She froze. The cat stopped purring. Total silence.

Helen crawled again, closer and closer. Her face drew level with the arm of the silent chair. She raised her head and peered over.

She gasped. She was face to face with a cat, certainly. But not their cat. Not the cat they wanted. Staring back at her from wide blue eyes, dark ears twitching, was a sleek, pencil-thin Siamese!

Seven

Stunned, Helen sat back with a bump. The Siamese cat stretched and stood up. She chose not to notice Helen sitting there, her mouth open. Instead, she leapt soundlessly from the chair and stalked towards the french doors. Long, thin tail in the air, head up, the pale yellow cat minced out on to the terrace.

Helen moaned. What else could possibly go wrong? She followed on all fours, planning to slip out of the house unnoticed. But all heads on the terrace turned at the Siamese cat's appearance. And soon Speckle's sharp eyes spotted Helen crawling after. He barked and tilted his head to one side.

'What was that?' Mark came back from the edge of the terrace.

'It's only Lady.' Mrs Saunders watched the elegant cat swish by. Lady chose a spot in the sun by the side of the pond, and sat staring at the giant goldfish.

'No, the dog's seen something else!' Mark went to peer inside the room.

Helen looked up at him. She stood up awkwardly. 'I . . . we . . . I thought . . . that is!' She spluttered and stammered. How do you explain what you're doing on all fours in someone else's house? She took a deep breath and waited for Mrs Saunders to go off and call the police.

But Mrs Saunders realised in a flash what had happened. She pointed to Lady, then turned back to Helen. 'Hello, you're the other twin! You thought Lady was your cat! Oh dear!' She smiled. 'I'm afraid not. What a pity!' She was kindness itself. 'You must be so worried about the little lost cat! After all, you were entrusted with looking after him. Oh dear!'

Helen stepped out on to the patio, straightening her hair and tugging at her T-shirt. She smiled self-consciously. 'You mean, you're not cross?'

'No, not at all. Come along, let's check with my

husband which way your cat went,' Mrs Saunders suggested. 'He might have a better idea than I do.' She turned to the gardener. 'Mark, would you check round the back? Try the garage and the stables; you never know!'

Cheerfully Mark went off to continue the search, while Mrs Saunders led the twins round the side of the house. 'Geoffrey!' she called. 'Come and meet two of our new neighbours.' She turned back. 'Now, which is Hannah and which is Helen? I expect people are always mixing you up. You must find it extremely annoying.' She laughed and chatted, while Speckle settled to wait. Soon, a tall important-looking man with grey hair came out to join them.

Yes, the black cat had made his way across the lawn, he told them. 'He went towards the paddock over there, over the wall and down towards the road.' Mr Saunders pointed out the right direction. 'The last I saw of him, he was poised on top of the bus-shelter. Perhaps you passed it on the way here?' He was less friendly than his wife, but not at all angry with them either. He tried his best to help.

Hannah was all set to move on. 'Thank you very much!' she said. 'We're sorry to bother you.'

'No bother.' Mrs Saunders smiled again. 'Twins! I've often wondered what that's like.'

'I hope you find your cat,' Mr Saunders said. 'If you go the side way, it'll be quicker.'

Relieved and grateful, the twins set off down a side path with Speckle. But just then the peace of the manor house was broken by a loud, unearthly cry. More a yowl than a miaow, more human than catlike, it came from the goldfish pond on the terrace.

'Lady!' Mrs Saunders recognised the Siamese cat's strange call.

'What's wrong with her now?' Mr Saunders frowned and set off at a trot towards the rumpus, closely followed by his wife.

The cat yowled again. There was the sound of something blundering against a flowerpot. Things crashed, there was a great splashing and hissing.

'Sin-bad?' Helen said slowly, disbelievingly.

'Oh no!' Hannah turned in her tracks. Together they ran after the Saunders.

They met Mark galloping round from the stable yard, an angry frown on his face. 'If that's my flower-pots, I'll strangle that flipping cat!' he threatened, running for all he was worth.

Crash! Crunch! Yowl! On the terrace, fur flew, a right royal fight had taken place.

They came on a terrible scene. Pots had toppled and crashed. Plants lay everywhere. Lilies in the pond rocked and bobbed on a stormy surface.

'My coy-carp!' Mr Saunders dashed to the edge of the pond and began to count furiously. Meanwhile, Lady had leapt out of reach of her invisible enemy, on to the head of one of the stone cherubs!

'Two-three-four!' Mr Saunders was on his hands and knees, peering below the surface. Giant, fat goldfish darted here and there in the gloom. 'Seven-eight!'

Mrs Saunders warned the twins and Speckle to stay back. 'They're Geoffrey's pride and joy!' she said, pointing to the fish in the pool. 'There should be ten of them in there.'

'. . . Nine!' The owner of Doveton Manor gave another cry.

The twins saw his nose touch the water. They waited. *Please, let there be ten!* Helen and Hannah prayed as one.

'. . . Nine . . . nine!' Mr Saunders looked in vain. He stood up at last. 'One missing!' he said, his voice hollow. 'It's Wellington!'

Mrs Saunders frowned. 'They all have names,' she whispered. 'Wellington is his favourite!'

From on top of the statue Lady yowled. She arched her back and spat.

Mr Saunders stood, hands on hips. He told Mark to run for the net to cover the pond, but he knew it was too late to save Wellington. 'I know who did this!' he said darkly. 'Lady would never touch the fish, we know that for sure!'

'Now, dear . . .' Mrs Saunders tried to be reasonable.

'Don't "Now, dear" me, Valerie! There's only one possible culprit in this case!' He ran back through events. 'It's that dratted runaway!'

Speckle whined at his angry voice. Lady hissed. The twins stood miserably among the broken plant-pots.

'He certainly went and did it!' Mark said. He turned on the twins, as if it was all their fault that his flowers were wrecked and Wellington was missing. 'That cat's in serious trouble if he did but know it.'

The twins didn't wait to find out what Mr Saunders would do next. Instead they made straight for the gates, with Speckle leading the way.

'Poor Wellington!' Helen shook her head as they

arrived in the village. 'I expect he made a tasty supper, though!'

'You don't mean . . . ?' Hannah stopped short.

'. . . A tasty supper for Sinbad?' Helen thought carefully. 'No, I still think he's innocent.'

'Then who . . . ?'

'. . . Would eat Wellington?' Helen asked. 'If not Sinbad, then who?'

'Exactly! That's what we have to find out.' Hannah faced facts. 'Because, unless we do, poor Sinbad will get the blame for this as well as for everything else!'

Helen agreed. 'And this time it's really serious. Mrs Saunders said Wellington cost an awful lot of money!'

They nodded firmly, full of determination to put Sinbad in the clear. Soon, they had to stop in the main street to let Speckle sniff around. 'That's it, boy!' Helen waited for him to pick up the trail. 'You know what,' she said, 'the village is against Sinbad, thanks to Mr Winter, but if he thinks he's beaten us, he's got another think coming!' Her fighting spirit came back full force.

Hannah agreed. 'Yes. What are we waiting for?' Helen's mood was catching. 'Come on, Speckle, let's go! Find Sinbad, boy! Come on!'

Speckle sniffed here and there, from one garden gate to another, between the two rows of pretty cottages that lined the street. The twins followed close behind.

Hannah's mouth was set in a determined line, Helen peered into gardens, underneath shrubs and bushes, under garden seats, along windowsills. Sooner or later, they would catch up with him and then set about finding out who had really eaten Mr Saunders' prize fish.

'Here!' Helen hissed. She peeped over a wall at a black shape asleep on a sunny lawn.

Hannah crept up beside her. She pulled Speckle along on the lead. 'This way, boy!' The dog didn't seem willing. She tugged again.

On the lawn, the cat woke and stretched. It showed the twins its white paws and belly. 'Oh!' Helen saw that it wasn't Sinbad. She frowned and marched on. 'Sooner or later!' she promised.

Hannah let Speckle go off on his own mysterious trail. The dog sniffed, trotted on, sniffed again. 'I think he's found something!' she called to Helen.

Just then, a door in one of the cottages burst open and stopped them all in their tracks. Mr Winter charged down his path. 'You two! I might have known!'

They stopped dead. 'What now?' Hannah stood in dread.

Mr Winter roared so loud that other doors opened. Down the street, Luke Martin came out of his shop to watch.

'You let that cat out on purpose, didn't you! I knew it!' Puppy darted out of the house, tangling himself between Mr Winter's legs. He barked and yapped at them for all he was worth.

Luke came up the street. 'What is it now? What's wrong?'

'Wrong?' Mr Winter was beside himself. 'Ask those two what's wrong! My fish supper, that's what!'

Hannah made a face at Helen. 'What's he on about his fish supper for?'

'Dunno, but I think we're about to find out!' Helen gritted her teeth.

'A lovely piece of fish! I drove into Nesfield especially to buy it! Rainbow trout, caught fresh today! Cost me the earth!' Mr Winter rushed into the street in his carpet-slippers, while his neighbours looked on.

Luke tried to calm him down. He stepped between him and the twins. 'Are you saying these girls took your fish, Mr Winter?'

'Not the girls!' he shouted. 'What would they want with it? No, it was that . . . cat!' The last word came out as a strangled cry. The old man was red in the face with fury.

'Again?' Luke raised his eyebrows.

'Yes, again! Exactly; again! My fish supper! It comes to something when you can't turn your back on a plate of fish for a single moment! I put it there on the window-ledge. Two seconds, my back was turned, and snaffle! The little brute got it! One fell swoop and it was gone! Just the empty plate left on the ledge, and that horrible black cat skulking off as fast as its legs would carry it! I saw him!' He paused for breath.

Luke whistled through his teeth. The neighbours tutted. Some went straight inside to clear the food from their tables. 'That's torn it,' Luke told the twins.

'Sinbad didn't do it!' Helen breathed, her faith in him unbroken. 'And we don't believe he stole Wellington from the pond either!'

'Shh!' Hannah warned. No point in involving Luke in that. Back up the street, she saw Mr Saunders and

Mark heading towards them. They must have decided to give chase, and the danger to Sinbad mounted by the minute.

Mr Winter spotted the local landowner and cut short his attack on the twins. Instead, he rushed to tell the two men about the latest disaster.

Quietly, Luke took the twins to one side. 'If I was you two, I'd make myself scarce,' he advised.

'You mean run away?' Helen asked.

'Yes. Vamoose! Scarper! Beam me up, Scotty! I wouldn't hang around in the present circumstances!' He watched Mr Winter discuss events with Mr Saunders.

Hannah knew Luke was on their side. He was their first friend in Doveton; the one who'd invited their dad on to the cricket team and lent them his ladders. She trusted him. 'Which way?' She got ready to run.

Luke scratched his bald head. 'That depends.'

'On what?'

'On whether you want to find Sinbad before they do.'

'Why, have you seen him?' Hannah cried.

He nodded. 'I did see a streak of black whip past the shop a couple of minutes back, yes!'

'Which way?' Helen tugged at his elbow. Speckle jumped up.

'Again, that depends. If you want to stay in one piece, that way!' Luke pointed up the fellside. 'But if you insist on trying to bring the villain to justice, you should try that way!' He pointed down a footpath that led to the lake.

'He didn't do it!' The twins began to argue, then thought better of it. 'Thanks, Luke!' They were on their way, towards the bright water's edge.

'Just one other thought,' Luke said.

'Hurry up! They're after us, look!' Helen saw that three angry men were bearing down on them.

'I should try Barbara Wesley's cottage first, if you really want to find Sinbad. She lives at Watersmeet, past Lakeside Farm. I'd like to bet that's where old Sinbad was heading; back home. See what I mean?'

The twins had no time to think. The men were only a few metres away, and still angry. Mr Winter raised his finger at them, ready to start all over again.

'Thanks!' Helen darted towards the path. 'Come on Speckle, Hannah!'

The three of them pelted down towards Lakeside Farm. From there, they would soon find Watersmeet.

'I only hope Luke's right,' Helen gasped. Her legs ached with running.

'Me too.' Hannah sprinted ahead, more determined than ever to save Sinbad from a fate worse than death.

Eight

The whole village came out to watch. The chase was big news in quiet Doveton; word went round that Mr Saunders, Mr Winter and Mark were on the warpath.

'Who are they after?'

'The Home Farm twins.'

'Aren't they looking after Miss Wesley's little black cat?'

'Yes, it's something about fish . . . !'

The neighbours gossiped on their doorsteps. They shook their heads. As a rule, Doveton was such a nice, genteel place. They watched in astonishment as Speckle led the merry dance down to the lake, with the twins hot on his heels.

'. . . Those girls are in for it when Mr Saunders gets hold of them!'

'I should think so too. Poor Mr Saunders worships those fish!'

Heads swivelled towards the landowner, the teacher and the gardener. There was much shouting and waving of arms as they discovered which way the twins had gone.

'. . . I'm glad I'm not in their shoes!' Heads shook, tongues tutted.

'Those coy-carp are worth a lot of money!' They blew up the affair of Sinbad and Wellington into headline news. 'Mr Saunders had that fish insured for two hundred and fifty pounds!'

'. . . And just look at Mr Winter! I never knew he could run like that!'

'. . . In his carpet-slippers!'

'And Puppy; look at him! Look at his little legs go!'

Gradually the action in the street died down. Only the most curious, a band of children and dogs, followed it down to the lakeside.

Helen and Hannah let Speckle lead them. Their legs were young, they easily outran the three men on their

trail. Their lead stretched to a hundred metres, two hundred. Soon they could nip out of sight down a short-cut through John Fox's farm.

'Mr Fox, have you seen Sinbad?' Helen yelled, waiting for the old farmer to appear.

His dog, Ben, barked from his kennel. The farmhouse door opened. John Fox peered out. 'He's not gone and given you the slip again, has he?' He stumped out in his socks and shirt-sleeves, sucking an empty pipe. 'The little devil!'

'Yes, and half the village is chasing him!' Hannah cried.

Mr Fox saw that things were urgent. He nodded at Ben. 'I've not seen the cat. But you can take Ben if you like. He can lend a hand.' He unleashed his champion sheepdog from the long rope. 'The more the merrier, eh?' He'd heard the rumpus of men shouting, climbing stiles, swearing to get hold of the cat if it was the last thing they did.

Ben bounded ahead with Speckle.

'What's the quickest way to Watersmeet?' Hannah gasped.

'The schoolteacher's place?' The old man blinked and scratched his stubbly chin. 'Down to the lake, turn left, follow the shore, it's the second house you come to!'

They yelled their thanks.

'And the best of British luck!' John Fox called. He turned to face three angry men approaching his yard. 'Now then, this is private property, you know!' He confronted them, barring their way through his farmyard short-cut.

'Good old Mr Fox!' Helen panted. This would give them a few extra minutes. 'Go on, Speckle! Go on, Ben! Find Sinbad, fetch!'

They ran and ran. The long grass scratched at their legs, insects and bright orange butterflies rose in the heat. The two dogs stormed ahead to the water's edge.

For a second, the twins halted as they came to the pebbly beach. The lake stretched before them, a bright blue. Here and there, pink and yellow windsurfing sails criss-crossed the surface. A white motorboat roared past in a cloud of spray.

'Turn left!' Hannah recalled Mr Fox's instructions. They set off again on weary legs.

'Follow the shore. Second house!' Helen gasped and panted. Pebbles scrunched underfoot. Ben and

Speckle loped ahead. To their right, the water stretched to a distant hilly shore; to their left, the land rose steep and rocky. Behind them, a band of men, children and dogs arrived on the beach.

'Quick!' Hannah spotted them. 'Look, there's the first house!' She read the name, 'Lake Cottage', on a wooden sign.

They ignored the low bungalow set against the hillside, and ran on.

'This is it!' Helen read a second sign: 'Watersmeet'. Speckle swerved to run up and down the little wooden jetty that stretched into the lake. He barked loudly. Ben followed him, then sat and waited.

Hannah took everything in. 'Watersmeet' was a small cottage with a big garden that reached almost to the water's edge. There was a fence, and a wooden gate arched with honeysuckle, a long lawn, and high flower borders. If Sinbad had come home, as Luke suggested, there were a thousand places where he could hide.

'Come on!' Helen took the plunge. She opened the gate and called Speckle from the jetty. 'There's nothing for it; we have to go in and look!'

The twins stepped into Miss Wesley's garden. They

sent the dogs scouting all around, through the bushes, around the back door of the house.

'Here's Sinbad's cat flap!' Helen pointed to the little metal door set into the wood. Her heart sank. 'What if he's inside the house? We'll never get hold of him then!'

Hannah could hear the scrabble of feet on the pebbly shore. Mr Saunders and his gang of helpers had reached Lake Cottage. She pressed the hinge on the cat flap. It stuck fast. 'I think Miss Wesley must have bolted it. Sinbad can't have got in there!'

They turned and looked frantically up and down the long garden.

Then Speckle darted towards a wooden shed standing in one corner. Ben followed. The two dogs rooted at the raised base of the shed. Speckle whimpered and turned to bark at the twins. Ben ran round the far side.

'They've found something!' Hannah dashed across the lawn. There was a shallow gap between the shed and the ground; room for cat to hide.

Helen flung herself full-length. 'It's dark under here! I can't see a thing!'

But Speckle's sharp bark told her to try again.

'Stay, Ben!' Hannah ordered. He guarded the other side. She knelt and crept forward.

'Yes, there!' Helen spotted a pair of huge green eyes. 'There he is!'

'Yes! We've got him cornered!' Hannah cried.

On the beach, the men drew nearer.

'Come out, Sinbad, we're here to help!' Helen reached under the shed. It was clammy. She put her hand on something cold and hard.

'Come on, Sinbad!' Hannah begged him to be good. 'For the first time in your life, please do as you're told!'

Sinbad hissed back at them.

'We want to rescue you!' Helen insisted. She felt amongst the damp leaves and stones. *Creepy-crawlies!* She shuddered and tried not to think about them.

'Look, Sinbad, the others will soon be here. Do you want them to catch you?' Hannah tried to talk sense into him one last time.

Sinbad hissed and growled like a tiger.

From behind the shed, Ben barked, deep and gruff.

Sinbad crouched in his dark corner. He judged his chances. Noise everywhere, eyes staring at him, noses snuffling, arms scrabbling; he was trapped.

'Sinbad, here, puss, puss, puss!' Hannah grew desperate. Mr Saunders opened the gate and strode up the lawn.

'Just come quietly!' Helen implored.

But Sinbad never gave in. He saw a gap between the hands and faces. He made for it with a stealthy, slinking movement. He met daylight, blinked, and made a run; out from under the shed, across the lawn, through the fence and on to the pebbly beach.

'Hey!'

'Watch it!'

'There he goes!'

'Oh, Sinbad!'

There was a chorus of cries. Speckle and Ben chased the cat. Puppy came up yapping and snapping.

Sinbad saw a forest of legs. He saw the empty wooden jetty stretching out into the lake, he spied a big log drifting by. Quick as a flash, he wove through people and dogs. Racing along the jetty, he took one almighty leap . . . and landed on the log.

There was a gasp. All heads turned to the lake.

'That was flipping amazing!'

'Wow, what a jump!'

'Look, he's floating away from the shore!'

'Did you ever see anything like it?'

They stood amazed and helpless as Sinbad drifted out of reach.

Nine

'Crazy cat!' Mark, the gardener, stood at the water's edge and whistled.

Sinbad balanced on the log. It bobbed and ducked on the water. 'Miaow!' he stared back at the crowd.

Helen and Hannah, Ben and Speckle ran into the shallow waves. Sinbad's log was already twenty metres out, and heading for deep, deep water.

Helen felt a hand on her arm. It was Mark. 'Don't go in after him,' he warned. 'It's not worth the risk!'

'But cats can't swim!' she cried.

Sinbad had arched his back. His fur stood on end.

He howled at them, and stared in horror at the water lapping all around.

'Hmph, he's no sailor!' Mr Saunders wrinkled his face to follow Sinbad's progress. A sudden silence fell. The dogs stopped barking, the crowd held its breath.

'He'll fall off!' Hannah breathed. A wave from a passing speedboat washed against the log.

Sinbad rocked and regained his balance.

'There goes one of his nine lives!' Mark said.

'What shall we do?' Helen stared at Hannah in horror.

Sinbad was drifting still further out. The log dipped and swayed. He miaowed helplessly.

'There's only one thing we can do,' Helen decided. She kicked off her shoes, ready to swim for it.

But the others stood in their way. 'Oh no you don't!' Mark said. 'You're not risking your necks!' he warned. 'Look, those speedboats are dangerous, if you did but know!'

A motor-boat roared in a great curve towards the shore. Its gleaming white hull cut through the water. The driver couldn't have seen Sinbad's log. Hannah waved frantically at him and he swerved away just in time.

The twins could hardly bear to look. The cat was on a collision course with danger. If one of those high-speed menaces came any nearer, or if Sinbad drifted our further, he would have no chance. Slowly, they opened their eyes and dared to look. The boat was gone; Sinbad was safe, for a few minutes at least.

'No heroics!' Mr Saunders warned.

Even Mr Winter seemed concerned. 'Perhaps the waves will wash the log back to the shore?' He stood anxiously on the jetty and watched Sinbad's rocky course.

But Speckle couldn't understand why everyone simply stood and watched. He ran back and forth along the shoreline, barking at the fast-disappearing log. He ran up to the twins, then along the jetty. He barked again at Sinbad, telling him to steer his log back to safety.

Another motor-boat roared close by. Its driver stared curiously at the crowd on the beach, while the twins waved and shouted like mad.

'Two lives gone!' Mark muttered through tight lips. He shrugged and looked down at his feet. 'We never meant this to happen to the poor thing,' he told the twins.

Just as things looked hopeless for Sinbad, and his cries grew fainter, his log wobblier, Speckle made a decision. He backed off and took a run along the jetty. He leapt into the lake.

'No, Speckle!' Helen cried out.

'Too late!' Hannah stared after him.

Speckle bobbed to the surface, his black head tilted back, his legs paddling furiously through the clear water. In the distance, another white boat sped towards them.

'What's he think he's doing?'

'Will he make it?'

'He's gaining ground!'

The onlookers held their breath as Speckle swam near to Sinbad's log.

On the shore, Ben saw what was happening. He yelped. He took a run into the water and out again. No youngster was going to show him up, he decided. He barked at Speckle and plunged into the cold lake, swimming furiously to catch him up.

They watched with bated breath as the two dogs drew near to the log. Sinbad, frozen with terror, stood with his back arched, his claws digging into the wet log. By now, the three animals were way out from the shore, and in the direct line of the motor-boat.

'Stop!' Helen cried. But her shouts were drowned by the roar of the engine.

'Watch out, Speckle!' Hannah shouted a warning.

It was no use, the sheepdogs were too busy rescuing Sinbad to notice the boat. Speckle had reached the log and swum behind it. He tipped at it with his nose, edging it back towards the shore. Ben joined him. Together they nosed it out of danger.

'Oh, good dogs!' Helen jumped in the air. 'They're pushing him back! Oh, brilliant!'

They saw Ben seize a broken stump that stuck out

from the log. He held it between his strong jaws, then he began to tow the log through the water. Speckle still nosed it from behind. Clinging fiercely to the top, Sinbad miaowed until he was hoarse.

Hannah saw that the curving course of the boat through the water would still bring it horribly close to the log. 'Speckle, Ben, watch the boat!' she yelled. Then she ran out on to the jetty and waved both arms. 'Watch out! Dogs in the water!' she screamed at the top of her voice.

The driver didn't hear, but he saw her in the nick of time. He cut his engine and drifted to a stop.

On the shore, everyone drew a huge sigh of relief.

'Well done,' Mr Saunders was quick to praise Hannah. 'Good thinking!'

Speckle and Ben swam on, tiring now, working hard to bring Sinbad back to shore.

They made it at last. Hannah charged into the water up to her knees. She stretched out and caught hold of one end of the log. Ben let go and waded on to the beach. Speckle pushed until he was sure that Sinbad was safe on dry land.

Hannah bent to lift the cat gently off the log. 'Come on, boy,' she murmured.

The cat, wet and trembling, collapsed into her arms.

His job done, Speckle left the empty log to be hauled ashore by onlookers. He followed Ben. Together, they shook themselves dry.

Helen ran towards them through the cold shower of water-drops. She flung her arms round their necks. 'Sinbad's safe!' she said, bursting with pride. She hugged them both. 'You two were brilliant. You saved his life.'

Ten

From that moment, Speckle stuck like glue to Sinbad's side.

If the cat couldn't look after himself, Speckle would be the one to do it for him. He came and fussed, poking his nose in as Hannah dried Sinbad with the hem of her T-shirt. Sinbad and Speckle touched noses; they were friends for life.

But the trouble wasn't over. As the crowd began to drift away, and John Fox came strolling down the beach to collect the other hero, Ben, Mr Winter worked himself up.

'It's all very well,' he said to anyone who would

listen. 'But there's no getting away from the fact that this cat's a thief!'

Mr Saunders frowned. 'Yes, there is that, of course.' He remembered Wellington, his favourite fish.

'A savage little thief!' Mr Winter pointed to Puppy's scratched nose. 'And what about my fish supper?' he challenged the twins.

Mr Saunders stepped in, and the two men discussed what to do next.

Helen's pride in Speckle and Ben began to fade, as she saw trouble still to come. 'What are we going to tell Miss Wesley when she gets back?' she muttered to Hannah.

Hannah added up the list of Sinbad's supposed crimes. 'There's stealing Speckle's breakfast and chasing the hens, for a start.' They'd seen that for themselves. 'Then there's nicking the cream from Dad's cake.' She counted the others off on her fingers. 'There's scaring Luke's doves and attacking Puppy!' *Which nobody saw*, she thought.

Helen nodded. 'They get worse. He did ruin Dad's photos!' No one could argue with that.

'Then there's Mr Winter's supper, Mark's flowerpots, and poor Wellington!'

'So they say!' Helen warned. 'But we don't believe that, Sinbad.' She put him down on to the smooth, dry pebbles. 'Look after him, Speckle!' She stood and waited with Helen for the two men to pass judgment.

Mr Winter cleared his throat. 'I'm sorry to have to say this!' he began.

'No, he's not!' Helen muttered.

'Shh!' Hannah trod on her toe.

'But we feel it's our duty to tell Sinbad's owner everything that has gone on in her absence!'

Helen groaned. A small crowd still stood there, enjoying the trial of Sinbad, the pirate cat. Only John Fox stood by with a deep frown, as the twins were grilled by the ex-headmaster.

'And of course, we must let your parents know about the damage the cat has caused!'

Speckle noticed Sinbad trying to slink away from the scene. Gently he nudged him back into place, close to the twins.

Two hundred and fifty pounds! Helen remembered how much Wellington was worth. She knew their mum and dad could never afford to buy Mr Saunders another carp.

Mum will never live it down! Hannah imagined that Miss Wesley would never want to speak to the family ever again.

'And!' Mr Winter laid it on thick. 'In my opinion, we should also inform the RSPCA about your inability to look after animals properly!'

'Oh, I say!' Mr Saunders coughed. 'I wouldn't go that far, surely!'

The threat hung in the air. But Helen's head went up. 'We did our best,' she said quietly. 'Sinbad's a bit of a handful, but he's not a thief!'

'Right. Innocent until proven guilty,' John Fox growled. He stared at Puppy, currently reared on to his hind legs, boxing Ben with his front paws, while the sheepdog stood quietly. Good training had taught him not to fight back.

'Puppy!' Mr Winter called him away. The Cairn Terrier wrestled on. 'Puppy!'

Mr Fox raised his eyebrows. Ben looked at him and waited for a signal. The farmer twitched his head. His dog trotted obediently home, leaving the terrier fighting the empty air. 'I wouldn't go chucking around accusations that you can't prove, if I were you,' he sniffed, before he stumped off home after Ben.

Helen and Hannah wanted to cheer. They set their heads high and waited once more.

'No more RSPCA talk, eh?' Mr Saunders looked uncomfortable. 'And let's pack up here, everyone. The show's over!'

Grumbling, Mr Winter had to agree.

They all trudged off the beach, up the path into Doveton; the kids with their dogs, the landowner and the schoolteacher, Hannah and Helen, with Speckle marching alongside Sinbad.

Mr Winter stopped at his own gate. He tugged Puppy on his lead. 'There's my missing fish supper,' he grumbled.

'We still don't think Sinbad did it,' Helen protested.

Hannah dug her in the ribs. 'It's OK, we'll pay for it from our pocket-money,' she promised.

As they went on their way, she stooped to pick Sinbad up. 'It's OK, Speckle, I'll carry him from here.' They walked in procession past Luke's shop and the cottages.

Then, when they arrived at the tall gates of Doveton Manor, they found Mrs Saunders waiting with the car.

'Jump in, Geoffrey,' she told her husband in a

cheerful voice. 'I rang the coy-carp people at the garden centre in Nesfield. They say we can drive over and choose another fish! Come on, get in, there's no use crying over spilt milk!'

She smiled at the twins as Mr Saunders got into the car. 'And, Mark, I've tidied up the flower-pots,' she went on. 'I rescued most of the flowers and re-potted them. The damage isn't as bad as it looks. Why not come with us and buy some new pots?'

The gardener looked relieved. Quickly he got into the back of the car, and they all drove off towards town.

Exhausted, Helen and Hannah sat down in the bus-shelter. 'Oh, Sinbad!' Hannah sighed.

The cat snuggled on her lap.

'How are we going to make them believe you're innocent?' She tickled his chin.

'That's what losing a few of your lives does for you!' Helen told him. 'You go all sweet and soft on us!'

'What a day!'

'What a weekend!'

'What a cat!' they said together.

'. . . What was that?' Helen leapt to her feet. A noise

split the silence. It came from the Manor; a squeal, a high cry, almost human.

Sinbad tried to leap from Hannah's lap. She caught him just in time. Speckle barked. 'It's Lady!' She recognised the angry yowl. She jumped up, as the racket on the terrace grew louder.

'It's another fight!' Helen ran to the open gates. 'Listen!'

More pots crashed on the stone terrace. They couldn't see clearly, but something splashed, and Lady set up a terrible row.

Hannah stared down at Sinbad, then up at Helen.

A light glimmered inside Helen's head. 'You know what?' she breathed.

'Are you thinking what I'm thinking?' Hannah whispered.

'You mean, if Sinbad's here . . . !'

'And Lady's in a fight up there . . . !' The cat yowled and spat, somewhere out of sight.

'Then that has got to be the real culprit!' Helen yelled. She began to race up the drive.

'Helen, wait!' Hannah ran with Sinbad. Speckle followed close behind.

They ran between the avenue of oak trees, then

leapt up the stone steps on to the terrace.

Yowl! Lady flew towards them, her mouth stretched wide open, uttering her terrified cry.

Helen dodged the cat. Hannah hung on tight to Sinbad. The Siamese darted from the terrace across the lawn.

'What on earth!' Helen stared at the scene. Garden statues rocked on their bases, flower petals blew here and there, water-lilies rocked on the pond.

Hannah too stopped short. Suddenly, in a flash, everything made sense.

They saw a huge grey bird perched at the edge of the pond. It flapped its wings, then settled. It peered into the fish-pond, its long, sharp beak poised ready.

'What is it?' Helen gasped. It was big, with long, stick-like legs, a tuft of grey on its head, and its beady eyes were fixed on Mr Saunders' fat carp.

'A heron!' Hannah recognised the beautiful bird. 'I think!'

Sinbad hissed from the safety of her arms, Speckle crouched. He waited for orders. Fascinated, the twins hunched behind a statue and watched.

The heron had his eye on his prey. Soon, any

time now, he would dart his sharp beak into the water, stabbing, grabbing another wriggling orange fish.

The twins knew they had to stop him. Here was their villain; the thief who had terrorised the village, doing what came naturally. He was a hunter, a fisher, a magnificent bird. And he had to be stopped.

Helen and Hannah stood up together. Speckle growled. The heron looked up with his haughty eye. He spotted them. Shifting on his long legs, he cocked his head to one side.

'I'll do it,' Helen whispered. Slowly she advanced across the terrace. She raised her arms at the heron.

Across the pond, he spread his mighty wings. The game was up; there'd be no more fish for supper tonight.

'Shoo!' Helen called. She was almost sorry that she had to scare him away.

The wings flapped, the long legs launched the huge bird into the air.

The twins watched him rise over the pond, overhead, across the lawn. He flapped and rose. He cast his shadow on the grass, then cleared the oak trees, rising higher. Soon he soared into the blue sky away from Doveton towards the lake and, tomorrow, to new hunting-grounds.

Eleven

'Sinbad didn't do it!'

'It was a heron, after all!'

Hannah and Helen rushed back to the village.

'Did you see him?' Helen cried, as Luke came to meet them. 'Did you see the heron? He was this big!' She stretched her arms wide. 'He was the one who caught Wellington! Did you see?'

Luke steadied her. 'A heron? Yes, that's right, one did just fly over.' A heron was a rare enough sight for people to come out and take a look. 'Fred Hunt popped in to tell me there was one about.'

Hannah cuddled Sinbad. 'Poor Sinbad, he got all the

blame!' She described how they caught the heron red-handed. 'He was after another of Mr Saunders' carp!'

'But you stepped in and saved the day!' Luke was impressed. 'Well done. I'll make sure the Saunders get to hear about this!'

'Oh, thanks!' Hannah beamed. Now their parents wouldn't have to fork out for Wellington. 'And you'll tell them that Sinbad's not guilty? He never went near the fish-pond!'

'Or Mr Winter's supper, I suspect!' Luke chuckled. 'Though that's something we could never prove!'

'Hannah and I knew it all along!' Helen was quick to point out. 'Puppy's nose and your doves, that must have been the heron too!'

Luke considered this, then smiled. 'You know what? I think this means that Sinbad's off the hook.'

Hannah gave the cat a little squeeze.

'Phew!' Helen leaned back and searched the sky for the heron. But he'd vanished from sight. 'He was this big!' she said again. 'And grey, with a white front. He looked really clever, like he could stand for hours on one leg, just waiting. Then he would pounce.' She mimed all the actions.

'They are amazing birds,' Luke agreed. 'And I'm glad it wasn't Sinbad.'

'But just look at him,' Hannah said. 'I knew Sinbad would never do anything really naughty.' Sinbad's sweet little face peered out from his mass of soft black fur. His rough pink tongue licked her fingers. He purred.

'Says you!' Luke laughed.

Miss Wesley's car was already in the farmyard. The shed door hung open and the hens strutted in and out. Sugar and Spice hopped happily inside their hutch, and Lucy and Dandy cackled from their field. Everything was normal, as the twins, Speckle and Sinbad made it home.

Helen ran to the shed and grabbed the door.

More slowly, talking softly to Sinbad, Hannah followed. 'Now, Sinbad, this is only for a few minutes. I have to put you back in here, and you can have a little nap. We'll be back in no time!' She eased him into the shed. Like a lamb, Sinbad went and settled on the red cushion.

Helen pulled a face. 'He's changed his tune!'

'He's being good!'

'Pity!'

'Why?' Softly Hannah closed the door on the purring cat.

'He was more fun when he was naughty!'

'Helen!'

She grinned. 'OK, come on, let's hope they haven't discovered that he went missing!' She led the way to the kitchen.

But they stopped short on the doorstep. Inside, their dad was chatting happily to their teacher.

'And are you sure Sinbad's been OK?' Miss Wesley asked. 'I was worried about him when I left you to cope. He can be very difficult!'

'Oh no!' David Moore waved his hand airily. 'He's been great.' He offered her the biscuit tin. 'Here, have a home-made chocolate-chip cookie to go with your tea.'

'Thanks. Are you sure about Sinbad?'

The twins took cover, as Miss Wesley glanced round the room looking for her cat.

'Absolutely positive!' their dad insisted. 'He's been the perfect guest!'

Helen and Hannah's jaws dropped. Then they clapped their hands over their mouths to stifle the giggles.

'And where is he now? Can I see him?' Miss Wesley stood and brushed the biscuit crumbs off her sweat-shirt.

'He's outside, safe and sound. I'll get the girls to fetch him.' David Moore sprang to his feet. 'Hannah-Helen!'

'Yes?' They popped into the doorway.

'Ah, there you are. Barbara's come to collect Sinbad.'

'Aah!' they sighed. 'Already?'

Miss Wesley smiled. 'You mean, you want to keep him a bit longer?'

Their dad stared at them from over her shoulder. He shook his head furiously.

'Forever!' the twins declared.

'Oh, I don't think you could do that,' he protested. 'After all, Barbara would miss Sinbad dreadfully, wouldn't you?'

She nodded. They sighed.

'Would you bring him here, please?' Half-hidden behind their teacher, their dad nodded for all he was worth.

So they skipped off, back to the shed, to find faithful Speckle on guard by the door.

Hannah patted him, then went in to collect Sinbad. All four went happily back to the kitchen.

'There you are, you little rascal!' Miss Wesley stretched out her arms. Soon she had Sinbad snuggling there. 'He feels a bit damp,' she said, looking puzzled.

The twins smiled back at her, saying nothing.

'Well, never mind. His basket's in the car.'

'I'll get it!' Hannah ran out again. She waved at her mum as she saw the car pull up after a long day at work. 'Miss Wesley's come to collect Sinbad!'

Mary Moore nodded. 'I saw her car. Is everything OK?'

'Fine!' Hannah gave her mum a bright smile.

They went in together.

Helen was telling them the story of the heron, minus the bits to do with Sinbad. 'He was this big!' she explained, spreading her arms even wider than before.

David Moore cut in. 'I was just saying; Sinbad can come and visit us again,' he told his wife.

'Any time!' Mary took a cup of tea and went and tweaked Sinbad's ear. 'He's a little cutie!'

Sinbad blinked and purred.

The twins smiled happily as Miss Wesley put Sinbad

in his basket to take him home. Speckle said a special goodbye. He pushed his nose under the lid of the basket and gave a little yelp. They all stood at the gate and watched the teacher drive him off to Watersmeet.

All evening, the twins wore their big smiles.

'What are you two so pleased about? What are you up to?' their dad asked suspiciously.

'Nothing!' Helen said. 'Honest!'

'We're feeding Sugar and Spice!' Hannah protested. She poured flakes of dried vegetables into a dish. The rabbits nibbled and chewed.

But their mum came across the yard with a puzzled frown. 'Helen-Hannah, what's my best red cushion doing in the shed?'

Hannah looked at Helen and blushed. 'Ah!' Their faces fell. 'I guess we should explain . . .'